MEI-MEI'S LUCKY BIRTHDAY NOODLES

SHAN-SHAN CHEN

ILLUSTRATED BY HEIDI GOODMAN

TUTTLE Publishing

Tokyo | Rutland, Vermont | Singapore

Published by Tuttle Publishing, an imprint of Periplus Editions (HK) Ltd.

www.tuttlepublishing.com

Library of Congress Cataloging-in-Publication Data for this title is in progress.

ISBN 978-0-8048-4461-1

First edition
18 17 16 15 14   10 9 8 7 6 5 4 3 2 1   1406TWP

Printed in Malaysia

Distributed by

North America, Latin America & Europe
Tuttle Publishing, 364 Innovation Drive,
North Clarendon, VT 05759-9436 U.S.A.
Tel: 1 (802) 773-8930
Fax: 1 (802) 773-6993
info@tuttlepublishing.com
www.tuttlepublishing.com

Asia Pacific
Berkeley Books Pte. Ltd.
61 Tai Seng Avenue #02-12, Singapore 534167.
Tel: (65) 6280-1330
Fax: (65) 6280-6290
inquiries@periplus.com.sg
www.periplus.com

Japan
Tuttle Publishing, Yaekari Building, 3rd Floor
5-4-12 Osaki, Sinagawa-ku, Tokyo 141 0032
Tel: (81) 3 5437-0171
Fax: (81) 3 5437-0755
sales@tuttle.co.jp
www.tuttle.co.jp

INTRODUCTION

It is so inspiring to see different races coming together to become one blended family. Biracial and multiracial families, parents who have adopted children from different countries, and families that practice many different cultural traditions—all of these communities add a wonderful depth and dimension to the world.

To celebrate this multicultural spirit, I turned to my love of cooking to create a story about an adopted Chinese girl named Mei-Mei who, with the help of her adoptive parents, learns about her Chinese cultural heritage through traditional foods. This book is about Mei-Mei's birthday. It is a tradition in the Chinese culture that you eat noodles on your birthday. The length of the noodles signifies a long and happy life.

Cooking and food are often the centerpiece of many families' memories. In our busy culture of instant gratification, children can miss the special experience of being in the kitchen with older family members. During these times, so much more than a meal is created—morals are taught, history is shared and bonds are formed.

My hope is that this story, with its step-by-step walk through the making of a traditional meal, will allow children to share in pleasure of celebrating a culture through its food. This book was written to foster an interest in cooking among a younger group of children through a story rather than a cookbook. The recipe is included so that children will be inspired to prepare the dish and share in the memory, and create a bonding experience.

Note: Please always supervise children when knives, hot liquids, and heat sources are being used. If you do not have a wok, you may use a frying pan. I hope you enjoy this book and create your own lasting memories in the kitchen.

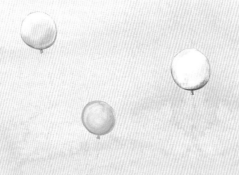

The sun is shining through Mei-Mei's window.

She hears the birds chirping loudly outside from the big oak tree.

Mei-Mei yawns and stretches her arms above her head.

She quickly jumps out of bed.

Today is Mei-Mei's birthday. She is turning six years old.

Mei-Mei runs to find her mom and dad.
They are still sleeping.

She jumps up and down on their bed
singing "Good morning! Good morning!"

Mom and dad wake up and sing
"Happy birthday, Mei-Mei!"

Mom asks, "Do you know why today is an extra special day for us?"

"Yes, yes, yes!" Mei-Mei shouts. "This is the day you and Daddy brought me home from China so we could be a family!"

"That's why your birthday is so important to us," dad says, and he gives Mei-Mei a great big hug.

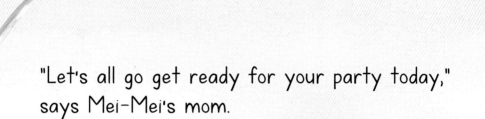

"Let's all go get ready for your party today," says Mei-Mei's mom.

Mei-Mei runs to the bathroom to brush her teeth and wash her face.

Then she runs down the hallway into her room to get dressed.

Mei-Mei goes to her closet and takes out her beautiful new red dress.

It has a large pink bow on the front.

She pulls the silky smooth fabric over her head and slips on her favorite shoes.

Mei-Mei twirls around in front of the mirror.

Her dress makes her feel like a princess.

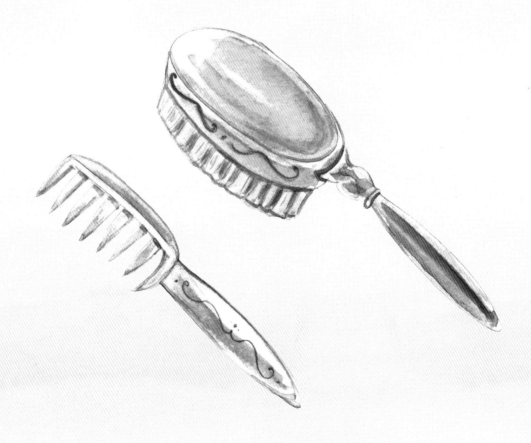

Mei-Mei hurries down to help her mom in the kitchen.

"Are we going to make the special birthday noodles?"

"Of course we're going to make the good luck noodles!" her mom says.

In the Chinese culture, it is a tradition to eat noodles when celebrating a birthday.

Noodles are eaten for good luck. They are long to symbolize a long and happy life.

Mei-Mei's mom has already pulled out all the ingredients from the refrigerator.

She starts to thinly slice the beef on the cutting board.

She asks Mei-Mei to bring her the wok from the cabinet.

"Which one is the wok?" Mei-Mei asks.

Mom explains that the wok is the large black cooking pan that has a deep round bottom which is shaped like a large bowl.

Mei-Mei finds the wok. It is very big and very heavy.

She uses all her strength to carry it over to the stove, placing it down with a loud THUD!

Mei-Mei's mom asks her to measure out
eight cups of water. Mei-Mei gets on a
step-stool and slowly pours the water
from the measuring cup into the wok.
Then she steps down and her mom turns
on the stove.

Mei-Mei watches the water until she sees
thousands of tiny bubbles floating to the
top. Her mom gently places the long yellow
egg noodles into the boiling water.

Mei-Mei's mom asks her to start
cleaning the mushrooms.

Mei-Mei gently wipes down each
mushroom with a damp paper towel.

Her mom explains that mushrooms are like sponges and that
it's important to keep them from soaking up water, which
would make them soggy.

Mei-Mei watches as her mom rinses the vegetables.

Mom chops the green onions, carrots, and bok choy.

Mei-Mei helps her mom pour the water out of the canned bamboo shoots.

Just then the timer goes off with a loud BUZZ.

Mei-Mei's mom puts on the oven mitts and takes the pot of cooked noodles and pours them into the metal colander waiting in the sink. All the heat from the hot water makes a big steam cloud in the air.

"Now we have to turn on the faucet and rinse the noodles with cold water to cool them down. This will stop the noodles from overcooking and getting too soft."

Mei-Mei watches as her mom pours some oil into the wok.

She hears the oil crackling and snapping as it starts to get hot.

Mom removes the beef from the bowl and puts it into the wok. She stirs the beef until it's a golden brown color.

"Do you want to help pour the vegetables into the wok, Mei-Mei? You have to be very careful when you are near the stove. The flames are very hot," mom says.

Mei-Mei stands on the step-stool and very slowly and carefully pours all the fresh vegetables in with the beef. She takes the wooden turner and mixes the vegetables.

Mom and Mei-Mei let all the vegetables simmer together and then mom takes the noodles and pours them into the wok.

She grabs two wooden spoons and mixes everything together. The stir-fried noodle mixture is called "chow mien."

Mom pours the chow mien into a big bowl. Mei-Mei cannot wait to eat it!

Soon, family and friends start to arrive. Nai-Nai and Yei-Yei hand Mei-Mei a red envelope.

In the Chinese culture, the red envelope symbolizes good luck and is given for special occasions. It is usually filled with money.

Mei-Mei says, "Shay shay! Thank you!"

Everyone sits down
around the table.
Mei-Mei is so
excited to enjoy
her birthday
noodles with
her family. Her
mouth is watering
with anticipation.

She grabs her
chopsticks and
carefully clicks the
two sticks together
to pick up the long,
warm noodles.

She puts them in her mouth and all the flavors melt together on her tongue.

Mei-Mei is so happy that everyone is here to wish her a happy birthday—and especially to share her yummy birthday noodles.

Today was a great day!

LUCKY BIRTHDAY NOODLES

Prep Time: 20 Minutes
Cook Time: 15 Minutes

INGREDIENTS:

$1/2$ lb. flank steak, thinly sliced across the grain

$1/2$ cup soy sauce, low-sodium soy can also be used

1 tablespoon sugar

8 fresh shitake mushrooms, thinly sliced

$1/4$ cup sliced green onions

1 cup chopped carrots

1 cup bean sprouts

$1/2$ cup bamboo shoots (canned and drained)

2 cups bok choy

1 cup beef stock

$1/2$ tablespoon cornstarch

1 tablespoon sesame oil

1 package 8 oz egg noodles

2 tablespoon vegetable oil

DIRECTIONS:

1. Combine sliced beef, sugar, soy sauce, and sesame oil in a bowl, and mix well.
   Set aside, and marinade for 20 minutes.

2. Dice the mushrooms, carrots, green onions, bamboo shoots and bok choy.
   Soak, rinse, and drain the bean sprouts.

3. Place 8 cups of water in a pot. Add egg noodles in boiling water for 6-8 minutes.
   Drain well and rinse with cold water.

4. In a separate bowl mix together cornstarch and 1 tablespoon water.

5. Drain the beef, setting the marinade aside.

6. Heat the oil until it sizzles, then stir-fry the beef for 3-4 minutes till golden brown.
   Place cooked beef onto a plate.

7. Pour the beef stock, beef marinade into the wok and mix well. Bring to a boil, and stir constantly.

8. Add all the vegetables and simmer for 3 minutes.
   Add cornstarch mixture and simmer 2 minutes till sauce is thickened.

9. Add noodles and stir, until all is hot.

Serve warm and enjoy. Beef can be replaced with chicken, pork, shrimp or tofu.

Acknowledgments

First and foremost, I would like to thank my wonderful husband Marcale and my two beautiful children Kymaya and Landon for inspiring me to write this book. You all joined in and were so encouraging when it was just an idea. Best of all is the time we spent together in the kitchen cooking and making memories. It's because of those moments that I wanted to put this story down on paper.

This book is dedicated to my parents Ven-Yung Chen and Guey-Fang Chen who instilled in me a love of Chinese traditions and told me stories about my culture—a legacy that I want to continue passing it down to my family and sharing with others.

I want to express my gratitude to the many people who saw me through this book; to all those who provided support, talked things over, read, offered comments, allowed me to read the book to their children and get feedback. Thank you for all your continued support. To my good friend, Heidi Goodman, thank you for reading the story and sharing in this dream through the beautiful illustrations that brought Mei-Mei to life.

And most importantly a huge thank you to Terri Jadick and Tuttle Publishing—without you this book would never have found its way to print. Thank you for trusting in me, believing in Mei-Mei and making my dream come true.

— *Shan Shan Chen Wallace*

I would like to thank my sweet, patient husband Jeff for his support and constant belief in my art, and my two crazy boys, Sebastian and Grayson for their (sometimes painfully) honest critiques of my work.

A huge amount of gratitude goes to my dear friend Shan Shan Wallace, who not only chose me to illustrate her beautiful story, but also encouraged me through every step of the illustration process. She believed in me, and so I believed in myself and was able to realize a childhood dream of becoming a Children's Book Illustrator.

Without Terri Jadick and her wonderful team at Tuttle Publishing, none of this would be possible, so I want to offer my sincerest thanks to them for giving Shan Shan and me (and Mei-Mei!) the opportunity to share our story.

Thank you to my friends/writers Marielle Leon, Ethel Brennan, Darrah Roberts and Poi Purl who took the time to read over the book in it's early stages and give us their feedback.

I dedicate my work in this book to my Grandmother, Virda Spurgin, and my best friend Trina Corson-Graham. You two have always believed in me, always loved me, and always been there no matter what. You have the qualities that inspire me to be a better person every day of my life.

— *Heidi Goodman*

The Tuttle Story: "Books to Span the East and West"

Many people are surprised to learn that the world's largest publisher of books on Asia had its humble beginnings in the tiny American state of Vermont. The company's founder, Charles E. Tuttle, belonged to a New England family steeped in publishing.

Immediately after WW II, Tuttle served in Tokyo under General Douglas MacArthur and was tasked with reviving the Japanese publishing industry. He later founded the Charles E. Tuttle Publishing Company, which thrives today as one of the world's leading independent publishers.

Though a westerner, Tuttle was hugely instrumental in bringing a knowledge of Japan and Asia to a world hungry for information about the East. By the time of his death in 1993, Tuttle had published over 6,000 books on Asian culture, history and art—a legacy honored by the Japanese emperor with the "Order of the Sacred Treasure," the highest tribute Japan can bestow upon a non-Japanese.

With a backlist of 1,500 titles, Tuttle Publishing is more active today than at any time in its past—inspired by Charles Tuttle's core mission to publish fine books to span the East and West and provide a greater understanding of each.

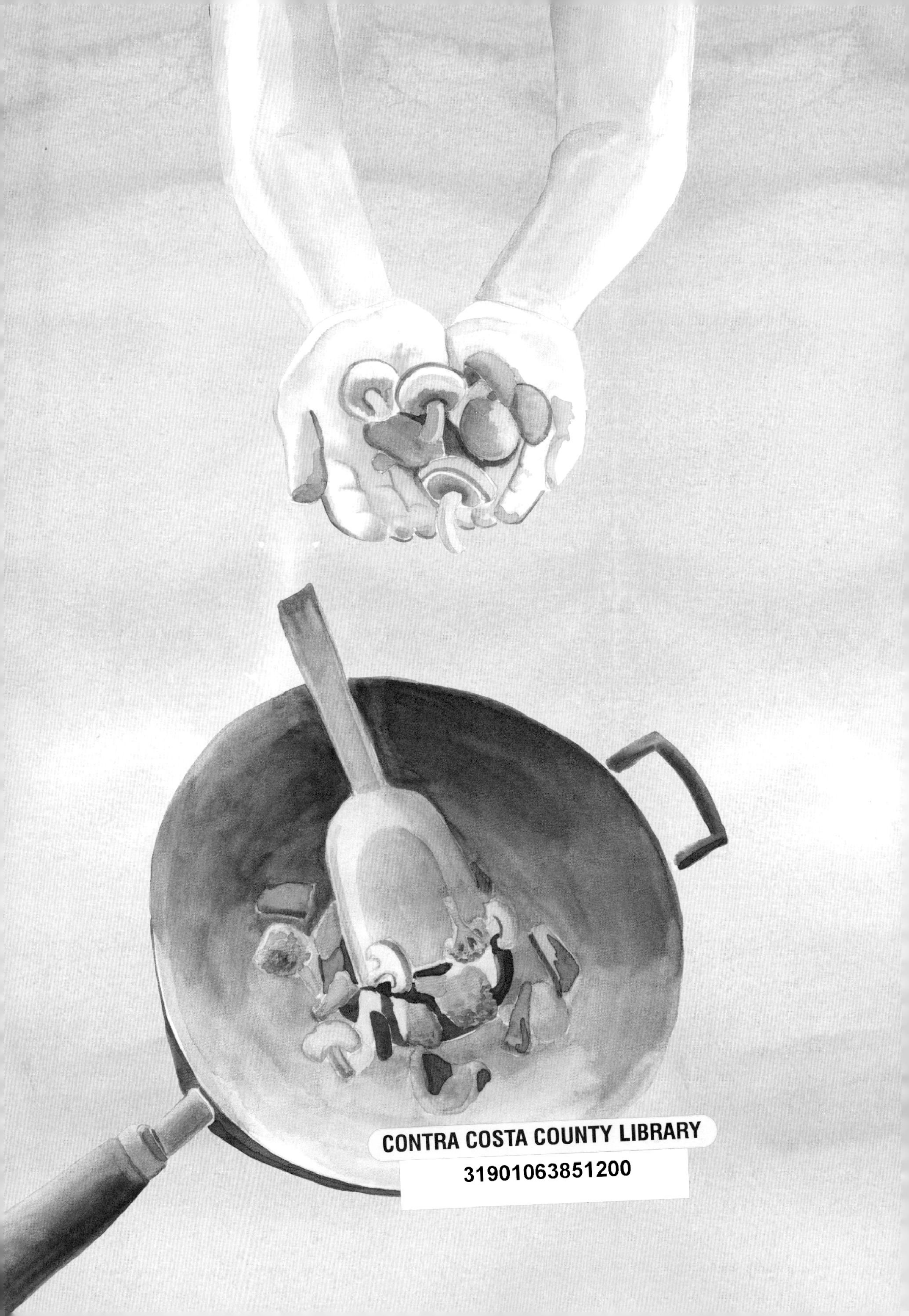